I0813883

by Grace Hansen

Abdo Kids Jumbo is an Imprint of Abdo Kids
abdopublishing.com

abdopublishing.com

Published by Abdo Kids, a division of ABDO, P.O. Box 398166, Minneapolis, Minnesota 55439.

Abdo Kids Jumbo™ is a trademark and logo of Abdo Kids.

052018

092018

Photo Credits: iStock, Science Source, Shutterstock

Production Contributors: Teddy Borth, Jennie Forsberg, Grace Hansen

Design Contributors: Dorothy Toth, Laura Mitchell

Library of Congress Control Number: 2017960571

Publisher's Cataloging-in-Publication Data

Names: Hansen, Grace, author.

Title: Light / by Grace Hansen.

Description: Minneapolis, Minnesota : Abdo Kids, 2019. | Series: Beginning science | Includes glossary, index and online resources (page 24).

Identifiers: ISBN 9781532108099 (lib.bdg.) | ISBN 9781532109072 (ebook) | ISBN 9781532109560 (Read-to-me ebook)

Subjects: LCSH: Light and darkness--Juvenile literature. | Light--Juvenile literature.

Classification: DDC 535--dc23

Table of Contents

What is Light?

Light is a form of energy.

Light can be made through heat. When **matter** heats up, it gains energy. One way it can get rid of that energy is to **emit** light.

The sun is very hot. It **emits** a lot of light!

Visible Light

Human eyes are very good at seeing light the sun **emits**. We call this **visible light**.

Light travels in waves. It is very fast! The waves are made by electric and magnetic fields. They have different **wavelengths**.

The energy of light depends on its **wavelength**. Humans see this energy as color.

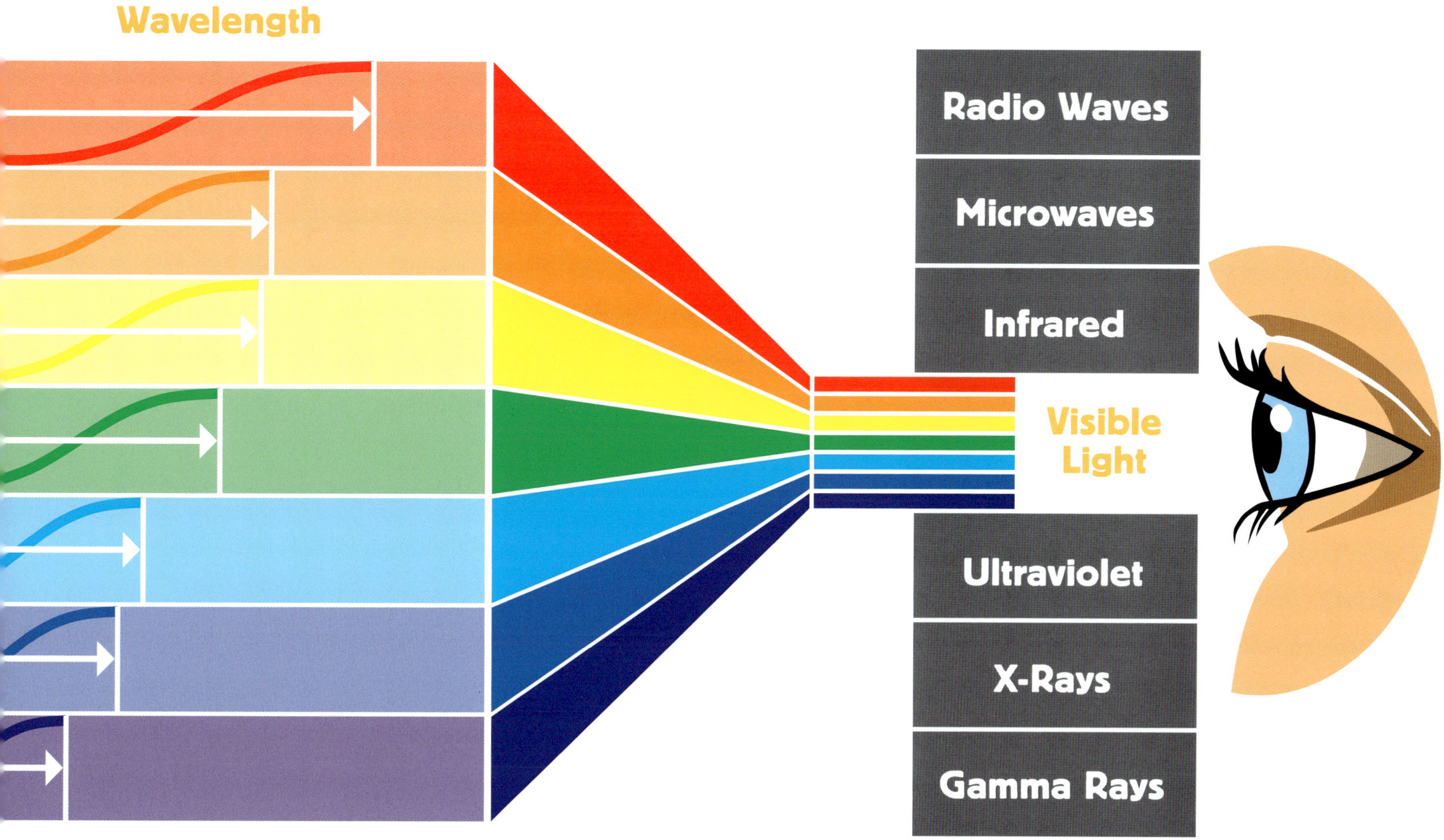

Wavelength

Radio Waves

Microwaves

Infrared

Visible Light

Ultraviolet

X-Rays

Gamma Rays

Shorter **wavelengths** have higher energy. The color violet has a shorter wavelength.

Longer **wavelengths** have lower energy. The color red has a longer wavelength.

Light is Waves & Particles!

Albert Einstein explained that light is not just a wave. It is carried by **photons**. This means that light is also a **particle**!

Photoelectric Effect

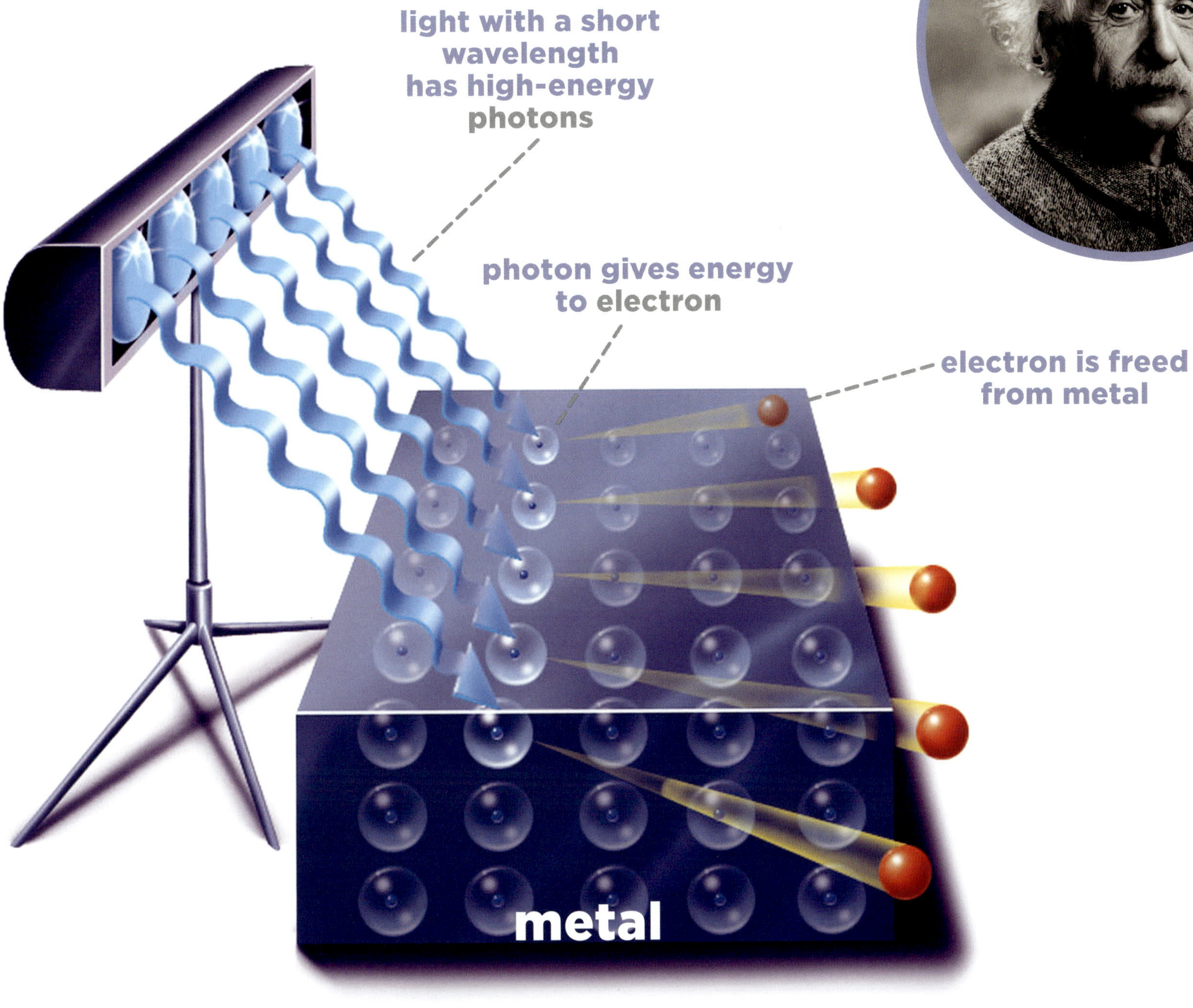

light with a short wavelength has high-energy photons

photon gives energy to electron

electron is freed from metal

metal

Let's Review!

- Light is both a wave and a **particle**.
- **Visible light** is energy we can see.
- Light travels very fast in waves that are carried by **photons**.
- The energy and color of light depends on its **wavelength**.

Glossary

electron – a very small particle that has a negative charge.

emit – to give off.

matter – all things that contain atoms and take up space.

particle – a basic unit of matter, such as a photon or electron.

photon – a tiny bundle of light with no mass or electric charge. It is the basic unit of light that acts like both a particle and a wave. It can interact with other particles.

visible light – the light humans can see within a certain range of wavelengths and frequency.

wavelength – the distance between two crests of a wave.

Index

Visit **abdokids.com** and use this code to access crafts, games, videos, and more!